Tall Tales of Old India from a Very, Very, Very Long Time Ago

CROWS AND OWLS
The Panchatantra Book Three Retold

Narindar Uberoi Kelly

Illustrated by Meagan Jenigen

For My Son Sean Uberoi Kelly

Order this book online at www.trafford.com
or email orders@trafford.com

Most Trafford titles are also available at major online book retailers.

Printed in the United States of America.

ISBN: 978-1-4907-4040-9 (sc)
978-1-4907-4043-0 (e)

Trafford rev. 07/07/2014

 www.trafford.com

North America & international
toll-free: 1 888 232 4444 (USA & Canada)
fax: 812 355 4082

Note To The Reader

I fell in love with these stories as a tween who stumbled across them in a library at a time when my family were refugees as a result of the partition of India between what is now Pakistan and India. I suppose part of the attraction of the stories was escape from the realities of being homeless in a part of India that seemed a different country, with people speaking different languages and eating food quite unlike anything I was used to. But the stories helped me by giving me some insight into what and why my parents were trying to teach me—and some appreciation for what I was resisting in a world turned upside down by our narrow escape from the violence and turmoil of our loss of home and country.

I decided I wanted my grandchildren to have access to these stories that meant so much to me, but in a language that they could easily understand. As I adapted the stories for modern readers, it occurred to me one of the great strengths of the Panchatantra (literally the five books) derives from what at first seems the sheer nonsense of listening in to animals talking like humans. Yet this absurd conceit of animals chatting and arguing and telling stories immediately establishes a strangely safe distance between the reader and these creatures. And even more strangely, we are transformed into observers and compatriots in their struggles with thorny issues of friendship, collaboration, conflict and ambition. If I was particularly taken with these tales at a time of vulnerability and uncertainty in my life, readers approaching and experiencing adolescence and young maturity (when does that process end?) are in some sense similarly adrift and puzzled by the strange new land of adulthood. Readers of these tales are assumed to be much like I was--expatriates operating in a new landscape they don't fully understand.

The genius of these stories is their relentless unwillingness to whitewash or romanticize adult life. They depict the ignoble as well as the noble, cruelty and deceit as well as honor, foolishness as much as cunning, deception as rampant as honesty. They show the underside as well as glimpses of fulfillment in adult life. The stories unveil the contradictory nature of adult life, its tensions, risks and dangers as well as its rewards. And it accomplishes this through the disorienting welter of stories within stories that pile up on each other to convey a kind of confusion that forms a powerful antidote to other literary forms designed to convey wisdom—like preaching, teaching, telling people what to do. Out of this confusion, somehow wisdom can escape as a form of deeper appreciation of the perils and tensions and value of leading a good life.

Narindar Uberoi Kelly

TALL TALES OF OLD INDIA

There was a king called Immortal-Power who lived in a fabulous city which had everything. He had three sons. They were truly ignorant. The King saw that they could not figure things out and did not want to learn. They hated school. So the King asked a very wise man to wake up their brains. The wise man, a Brahmin named Sharma, took the three Princes to his home. Every day he told them stories that taught the Princes lessons on how to live intelligently. To make sure they would never forget he made them learn the stories by heart. The third set of teaching tales Sharma told were:

Crows and Owls

Sharma began:

"Even if you are reconciled
Never trust an enemy
The Owls had their cave burned
When fire-wielding Crows arrived".

"How come?" asked the three Princes, and Sharma told this story.

CROWS and OWLS

The Panchatantra Book Three Retold

Narindar Uberoi Kelly

Illustrated by Meagan Jenigen

Crows and Owls

Introduction

The purpose of these stories has always been to teach basic knowledge and wisdom that makes for a better life. Each of the five 'books' in the original were organized around a theme: Loss of Friends, Making Friends, War or Peace, Loss of Gains, Ill-considered Action.

Book Three, here titled simply as Crows and Owls, covers how to deal with conflict when the stakes are high, how to prevent enemies from growing too strong and, when faced with strong enemies, how to consider an array of strategies open to you: from negotiating a peace to going to war if necessary, retreating, standing your ground without regard to consequences, making alliances or deceiving your enemies.

The main lesson: never trust an enemy. Above all, be cautious and always on your guard. Learn the dangers of foolish decisions, failure to keep secrets, betrayal, corruption, deceit and stupidity, because prudence in dealing with enemies and one's own counselors is more important than valor. One must discern the dangers and advantages of conciliation, the risk and rewards of self-sacrifice, the differences between true and false friends, the critical importance of planning and the courtesy due to, as well as the special danger of, an enemy who comes as a supplicant.

The *frame* story describes the life-long enmity between Crows and Owls, how it arose and how the Owls got strong without any action on the part of the Crows. Eventually the Crows decide to fight back. Both the Crow King and the Owl King consult trusted counselors and they give him advice on how to proceed illustrated through tales that form most of the book's *stand-alone* and *nesting* stories. These are separated in this presentation from the main or frame story about the struggle between Crows and Owls by a simple conceit: the right hand pages of the open book contain the nesting stories and the left pages carry the main or frame story of the Crow-Owl conflict. The text of the frame story is enclosed within a 'frame'. This allows parents reading aloud to young children, or young adults, or adults of any age, to choose how they want to read the book: frame story only, selected stand-alone stories, or sequentially left to right on the open pages to experience the original design of the whole book of stories.

Meanwhile *the frame story of the two adversaries continues on the left hand pages* and can be read without interruption of the nesting stories. For the purists, the book can be read in its entirety left to right on the open pages to experience the original design of this book of stories.

A word of caution: some of these stories illustrate Indian practices of many centuries past. Women are not often depicted or treated well, a phenomenon that continues to this day. But the stories have much to tell us. I trust that parents will help their children to understand the age-old realities described in the five books and use the occasion to teach their own values.

Crows and Owls

There was a large city called Earth Valley surrounded by hills. At one edge of the city, there was a sprawling banyan tree. In its dense branches lived a colony of crows and their King named Spirit. Not far away, in a cave, lived a rival King, a great owl, named Valor, who held a life-long grudge against crows. Whenever he met a crow he would kill him. He had killed so many over the years that there was a ring of crow skeletons around the trunk of his tree.

Eventually, the crows realized they had to do something. *They had allowed an enemy to progress without taking any action to stop it.* So King Spirit summoned his counselors. "Our enemy is proud and vigorous and attacks at night when he can see and we cannot. We can't counter-attack in the day because we don't know where his fortress is located. *There are six ways of proceeding: try to negotiate a peace, go to war, retreat by changing our base, take a stand without care of consequences, make alliances with others if possible, try duplicity by sowing discord in enemy ranks.* What do you advise we do?"

King Spirit had five learned and trustworthy ministers of long standing: Live-Again, Live-Well, Live-Along, Live-On, Live-Long. Each gave his advice and each recommended a different course of action. "*One should not go to war with a powerful enemy. Make peace instead*" said Live-Again. "I disagree" said Live-Well. "*This enemy is cruel, greedy, without principles. You should fight him.* If you try to make peace he will continue his piecemeal violence. *He may seem the stronger, but the small often slay the bigger with determination and energy.*" When asked for his advice, Live-Along disagreed with both Live-Again and Live-Well. "*The enemy is strong and vicious so you should neither make peace nor wage war. Change your base position.*" Then King Spirit turned to Live-On who said "I disapprove of peace, war, and especially change of base. *A crocodile can beat an elephant but away from his natural habitat he is at a total loss. Stay entrenched at home, stand firm resolved to do or die.* That is where glory lies." Live-Long had yet another recommendation. "*Seek an alliance with another group for there is strength in numbers even if each is not strong by himself.*"

Having heard each counselor out, King Spirit then turned to a very wise old retainer named Live-Strong who had advised the King's father. "Sir, I asked you to sit in our strategy session so you could hear what my counselors advise. Now I ask you to teach me the best action to take." Live-Strong took his time before replying respectfully "Your Majesty, while all the proposals thus far have merit, the present situation requires duplicity, double-dealing. You *cannot afford to be truthful and open to an enemy, even a former enemy, or a false friend. You must always be vigilant for a vulnerable point of the enemy.*" "But how can I discover vulnerability if I do not know his residence?" asked King Spirit. Then Live-Strong told him how to *spy on a foe through his functionaries to whom important duties have been delegated. One engages spies to sow intrigue and discord among important groups like counselors, chaplains, commanders, princes, tax assessors and the like. But one must also be wary of people like the royal household, the courtiers, the chamberlain, and various types of purveyors in one's own camp who can be easily corrupted.*"

"Sir," asked King Spirit "how ever did the deadly feud between crows and owls start?" and Live-Strong told this story.

Birds Pick A King

Once upon a time all types of birds gathered together: swans, cranes, herons, doves, pigeons, partridges, swallows, sparrows, cuckoos, woodpeckers, peacocks, parrots, cardinals, blue-jays, goldfinches, skylarks, sand-pipers, eagles, falcons, vultures, penguins, pelicans, owls, and many, many, others. They gathered together because they were concerned about not having a King Protector. They said "We have always thought of Garuda as our King but he is really God Vishnu's bird and serves him first and pays little attention to us. We need a Bird-King Protector who will defend us properly."

During this discussion, many of the birds noticed a wise old owl sitting quietly among them and, without thinking things through, asked him to be their king. They then proceeded to make the arrangements for a very big and very fancy coronation. When everything was just about ready, the owl was all decked out in royal robes and sat upon a handsome throne awaiting the ceremony to begin. Just then a large black Crow flew in with a very loud squawk and alighted right in the middle of the podium. When the other birds saw him, they whispered to each other "the crow is the shrewdest among all birds. Let us ask him his opinion of what we are about to do." So they said to the Crow "You know, the birds have no King Protector. So we unanimously decided to ask the owl to be our king and are about to crown him. What do you think?" The Crow laughed. "This is foolish. He is mean and ugly looking and blind in the daytime. Why would birds who see in the day want a king who can only see at night? Besides, Garuda is the king. A second king is not a good idea. After all, Garuda's very name keeps birds safe up to a point because everyone knows he serves God Vishnu himself and therefor has powerful friends. Remember, even feigning a message from the Moon helped the rabbits live in comfort." "How so?" asked the birds, and the Crow told this story.

How the Rabbit Fooled the Elephant

There was an Elephant-King who had four tusks and ruled over a very large herd of elephants. One time, during a twelve-year drought, all the tanks, ponds, swamps, and lakes in his area began to dry up. The poor elephants said to him "O King, our children are thirsty and some are even near death. Help us find water." So the Elephant-King sent scouts far and wide and in all directions to search for water. They eventually reached a lovely crater lake with clear blue water that all creatures who lived near it enjoyed. It was full of water-dwellers but its shore also supported many, many animals from small to big, including a colony of rabbits. The elephant scouts hurried back to tell the Elephant-King about their find. As soon as he heard about the lake, the King left to get to it as fast as he could with his large and slow-moving herd. When they reached the shore of the Lake of the Moon, the elephants plunged right in creating havoc along the edge of the lake. Once they had their fill they returned to their home area until it was time to get water again.

Unfortunately, the elephants destroyed more than the lakeshore. They had also destroyed the warrens of the rabbit colony that existed on that lakeshore for a long time. Many rabbits were killed in the stampede. The surviving rabbits gathered together to figure out what to do. The Rabbit-King asked the help of his most respected counselor named Victory who had served him well for many years. "I cannot go myself" said the King "but I want you to go as my emissary. You know all the facts. Speak with respect, reflection and full measure, as if you were me speaking. Make the best arguments that will help save us from further calamity." So Victory left and saw the Elephant-King had already started on the return journey to the Lake of the Moon. He seemed invincible surrounded by his strong elephant retinue. Victory climbed up a high and scraggly pile of rocks and from there addressed the Elephant-King. "Hope all goes well with you, your Majesty" and the Elephant-King asked "Who are you?" Victory answered "I am an envoy." "An envoy in whose service?" "I am in the service of the blessed Moon." "State your business" said the King. "As you know, your Majesty, no injury can be done to an envoy on business, so I may speak freely. By command of the Moon, I am here to say that you have done violence to the Moon's subjects who lived beside the Lake of the Moon, his lake. You may not know your own and your follower's strength, but you have destroyed a whole colony of rabbits, despite the fact everyone knows a rabbit lives with Lord Moon. Do not go to the Lake again or my Lord Moon's light will be withheld and you and your companions will perish." On hearing Victory's speech the Elephant-King realized his unwitting blunder and said "Please point me to where I must go to ask the blessed Moon's pardon."

Victory then took the Elephant-King to a different part of the Lake and showed him the Moon reflected in its clear water. Where upon the Elephant-King tried to purify himself by sucking up the water with his huge trunk. As he did so, the water was disturbed and the reflection of one Moon became that of hundreds of Moons. Victory cried out "Woe to you! You have enraged the blessed Moon. You should not have touched this Lake's water!" The Elephant-King pleaded "Please, Sir, please ask forgiveness on my behalf and I promise never to come near this Lake again or let my followers do so."

"That is why I think the birds should not choose the Owl as King" said the Crow. "The Owl would be a sly judge and you should expect betrayal rather than protection. Remember how the rabbit and the partridge died confiding in the Cat." "Tell us" begged the birds, and the Crow told this story.

Umpire Cat and His Ruling

"At one time of my life" began the Crow "I lived in a maple tree in a city park. Underneath the same tree also lived a partridge. We liked each other and spent a lot of time together. One day the Partridge went in search of food with his other friends and did not return. I was quite concerned and when a month had gone by and he did not come back, I was sure he had had some kind of mishap and died. I grieved for my friend.

"More time passed and a rabbit made his home in the hole which was right next to the Partridge's nest. I didn't object. But soon thereafter the Partridge showed up. He seemed very well fed and in good spirits and glad to be back home. When he saw the Rabbit, he chastised him for occupying his home. "Please leave as soon as possible" he said to Rabbit who replied "You are so wrong. You can call a place yours only while you live in it." "OK. OK. Let us ask our neighbors. I will abide by their testimony" said the Partridge. But the Rabbit argued "Even if your neighbors agree that you lived here for ten years, the place does not become yours, for that is the rule among men. For birds and beasts, possession is ownership. The place was unoccupied when I moved in, so now it is mine." "Clearly, we must go to arbitration" said the Partridge. So they took off to find a suitable umpire. Soon they ran into a cat who was a confidence trickster. It was only a matter of time before the Cat had both adversaries drawn into believing that he would be an impartial arbitrator. Still, the Partridge did not want to get too close to a natural enemy. But to make a long story short, the rogue Cat won their confidence completely and they got too close to him. He injured them both with one vicious swipe and quickly caught one in his teeth and the other in his claws. He killed and ate them both."

"If you" continued the Crow, "make the Owl a second King, just think he cannot see in the daytime, so what kind of Judge will he be?"

All the birds flew off to their homes and only the Owl sat on his throne awaiting a coronation for he was blind by day. He called out "What is this delay? Where is everybody?" Only his mate heard him and replied "Dear Owl, the Crow managed to find a way to stop the ceremony. All the birds have gone home. Only that Crow is still here. Let's go home. I will help you."

The Owl was deeply hurt and disappointed. He said to the Crow "You have wronged me grievously. I won't forget this. A cruel and ugly speech wounds so deeply that it never heals." Then he went home.

"Oh dear", the Crow reflected "I have made an enemy needlessly. I should have considered the consequences before I spoke the harsh truth when asked for my opinion."

"OK" said King Spirit "having inherited a feud among crows and owls, what can we do now?" Live-Strong said "I will have to deceive the enemy to conquer him just like the con man who robbed the Brahmin for his goat." "How so?" asked King Spirit and Live-Strong told this story.

How the Brahmin Lost His Goat

There was once a pious Brahmin who was the keeper of the fire and had the job of making periodic animal sacrifice to it. In the middle of the winter with the new moon due, the Brahmin went to a neighboring village to beg for an animal to sacrifice. A rich farmer gave him a well-fed goat that he tied up and swung onto his shoulder to take home.

On the way back, he ran into three cold and hungry wastrels who immediately saw their opportunity and plotted to get the goat from the Brahmin. They first passed him by, but later one, having changed his appearance, reappeared and said "Holy Sir, why are you carrying a dog on your shoulder? You know a dog is an unclean animal and pollutes you." The Brahmin was truly offended and replied "Are you blind? You think my goat is a dog?" "OK" said the rogue, no need to get angry" and went on his way.

Further along the road, two of the rogues, disguised, appeared and said to the Brahmin "Dear Sir. Even if the dead calf was your pet, you should not carry it on your shoulder. It defiles you." The Brahmin got more irritated and said "Are you blind? You call my goat a calf?" "OK. No need to get angry" said the two rogues. "Do whatever you want" and went away.

When the Brahmin was getting near his home village, the three rogues, disguised, appeared yet again and said "You know Sir, carrying a donkey on your shoulder is most improper. You must drop it and go bathe and cleanse yourself at once." Totally confused by now, the poor Brahmin, thinking that he carried some kind of demon that kept changing its shape, dropped the goat and made for home in a hurry. Of course, the three scoundrels had a feast of goat.

Having finished the story, Live-Strong continued "Everyman can be cheated by clever rogues. Also, it is better to cheat and avoid a quarrel with a crowd than pick a fight, for even if each member in it may be weak, an angry crowd is fearsome. Remember, the ants that ate the giant snake?" "How was that?" asked King Spirit, and Live-Strong told this story.

How the Angry Ants Ate the Giant Snake

A giant black snake lived in a huge anthill. The ants were used to his comings and goings via a large tunnel. But one day he tried to crawl along a much narrower hole and got injured for he was too big and because fate willed it. The ants quickly smelled the odor of new blood and crawled all over the snake which made him frantic. In his thrashing around he crushed and killed lots and lots of ants. They became very, very, angry and gathered in a huge crowd. By acting together they stung the snake all over and endlessly and kept enlarging his wounds until they killed him.

*

After finishing the story, Live-Strong continued "King Spirit, I have something to tell you which you must consider very carefully. We must use deceit as a device to vanquish the Owl-King. Conciliation, intrigue, bribery and fighting will not work. You must pretend to completely turn against me, rail loudly about my faults and the bad advice I have given you, hit me and smear me with blood, and basically leave me for dead at the base of our banyan tree. Then take all your crow retinue with you and fly off to Buffalo Mountain. You should stay there until I can win the trust of our enemy, find out the location of their fortress, and destroy it. You must not feel any pity for me or try to stop me. For *while kings need to treat their servants well, even pamper them, when it comes to war, they must let them live or die in battle.*"

King Spirit heard him out and then did exactly what Live-Strong wanted him to do. By this time it was getting dark and the owls were out and about. A scout owl had come near the banyan tree, saw the badly hurt Live-Strong at the base, and quickly flew back to the Owl-King with the news.

The Snake Who Paid in Gold

Once there was a Brahmin who worked very hard and put in long hours. But his farm remained very unproductive. Towards the end of one summer, when he had been dozing under a tree, he saw a fearsome snake with full extended hood looking directly at him from a nearby anthill.

Although scared, the Brahmin thought perhaps the Snake was the guardian of his field and he had never paid him any honor. Perhaps that was why the field was so unproductive. From now, he said to himself, I will honor him. So he got a saucer of milk from his home and presented it to the Snake saying "Guardian of my field, I am sorry I did not know. I have paid you no honor. Please accept my offering and show your grace to me." The Brahmin then went home.

The next morning he found a gold coin where he had left the saucer full of milk. He was very happy and from then on he left milk for the Snake every day and every morning the Snake left him a gold coin. After a few weeks had passed the Brahmin had to go to a neighboring village to get seed and told his son to take the saucer of milk to the Snake which he did as requested. The next morning, however, when he saw the gold coin, the greedy boy decided to kill the Snake and take the Snake's entire hoard of gold which he was sure would be nearby. The Snake did not die when the boy tried to kill him and instead attacked the boy and bit him on the neck. The boy died.

When the Brahmin returned and found out what had happened he could only say "One should always be generous to all living creatures or your own life will slip away. Remember the swans and their Lotus Lake nest?" "How was that?" asked the Brahmin's family, and he told them this story of the unfriendly swans.

Seeing an opportunity, the Owl-King got his retinue together and organized a massive crow-hunt. With a harsh battle-cry they flew to attack the crows in the banyan tree but found it completely empty of crows. "Better search for the crow line of retreat and kill them before they reach safety" the Owl-King ordered. Live-Strong heard the Owl-King and realized that it was time to draw their attention, for if they left, he would not be able to put his plan into action. So he squeaked feebly but loudly enough to alert the owls to his position. They quickly found him and took him to their king. He was able to explain "I was punished severely by my master because I advised that the crows not pick a fight with as strong an enemy as you are. Please help me and I will lead you to the crow retreat."

The Owl-King consulted his counselors as to what they should do. The first, an advisor named Red-Eye, said immediately "Kill the crow. It is best to kill an enemy before he can recover and gain strength. A lost chance brings a curse." "How come?" asked the Owl-King, and Red-Eye told this story.

The Unfriendly Swans of Lotus Lake

Once there was a King named White Lotus who owned a beautiful lake named Lotus Lake after him. Many rare golden swans had made their home in the Lake and people left them alone at the King's command because each swan paid him a gold tail-feather every six months.

As time went by, a gorgeous, glittering, large gold bird arrived at the Lake. The Golden Swans immediately challenged him. "You cannot live among us on this Lake for we rent all of it from the King by paying a gold tail-feather every-six months." The Gold Bird replied "You are very rude and unfriendly. I will not be any trouble to you." But the Golden Swans were adamant so the Gold Bird offered to go talk to the King himself. "What can the King do?" they said. We give lodging to no-one." "You really are very impolite. I will go tell the King" said Gold Bird. "When the King heard about the behavior of the Golden Swans, he ordered his servants to kill all of them and have a great feast. One wise Golden Swan who saw the King's guard arriving told the rest of the flock of Golden Swans that they would be destroyed unless they immediately fled the scene, all together, which they hurriedly did."

*

Next morning the Brahmin again took the saucer of milk to the Snake in his field and tried to win back his trust. "My son met the death that fit his intelligence." The Snake replied "*You cannot break a heart and then hope to repair it because the ache lives on forever*".

The Owl-King turned next to another counselor named Fierce-Eye. What is your opinion?" "Please don't listen to heartless advice" answered Fierce-Eye. *"One does not kill a supplicant.* The Dove paid due honor to his mortal enemy who came as supplicant to his door and died for it." "How was that?" asked the Owl-King, and Fierce-Eye told this story.

The Doves' Sacrifice

There used to live a cruel and vicious bird-hunter, a fowler, in a forest where all the birds lived in constant fear of losing their lives. The Fowler daily roamed the woods with his snare, net, cage and cudgel always looking to catch and kill.

One afternoon in high summer he was caught in a violent storm that completely drenched him and he sought shelter under a tree. He prayed for good fortune for he was cold and hungry. In the same tree lived a pair of turtle doves who loved each other truly and faithfully. Before the storm, the Dove Wife had been caught by the Fowler and lay tied up in his net. The Dove Husband was miserable for his wife was missing and he was bemoaning his bad fortune. "The house is not a home when the mistress is missing. My wife was my true love."

The ensnared Dove Wife heard her husband and called out "You are my loving husband and my very life. Listen please to my difficult advice. Our enemy, the Fowler, lies at the bottom of our tree in need of food and shelter. Do not let your hate get the better of you. He caught me for my sins, but you must help him."

The poor broken-hearted Dove Husband controlled himself and went and found an ember from another's fire and started a bonfire for the Fowler so he would stop shivering. But the Dove Husband had no food to give. In his love for his wife and in despair of his situation, he gave all he had left to the Fowler: he sacrificed his own body for his guest's meat.

When the Fowler saw the sacrifice, he was so ashamed of the life he had led that he vowed to seek virtue no matter the cost. He freed the Dove Wife. But when she realized her husband was gone, she grieved for him. "I cannot live without my love, my sweet husband." And she walked straight into the fire. As she did so, she saw a blinding light and her husband awaiting her in lordly shining garments with his arms wide open. She went right into them and the two flew straight to heaven for a long, loving and blissful life together.

The Fowler, faced with the self-sacrifice of the turtle doves, could not stop himself. He too walked into the burning bush and cleansed away his sins to also reach heaven.

*

Having heard the story, the Owl-King turned to his trustworthy counselor and asked "Flame-Eye, what should I do?" and the counselor recounted this story.

The Old Man Who Married a Young Wife

A rich old merchant lost his wife and decided to marry a young wife. Of course, no young girl wants to marry a very old man, so he had to pay a heavy price to a penniless shopkeeper to marry his young daughter.

As one would expect, few people love those who are old, even a son pays little honor to a doddering old father. Anyway, the young girl wife always averted her face from her husband when she lay in bed with him. But one night she suddenly turned towards him and hugged him tight. Oh ho! What's happening here thought the old man even as he thrilled to her touch. So he looked around very carefully and saw a thief cowering in a corner of the bedroom. My wife embraces me for she is afraid of the thief. So the old man said to the thief "Thank you. You are my benefactor. Take whatever you like." "Actually, there is little here I want to steal. But if I want something I will return, and I *will* return if your wife will no longer cling to you!"

*

"Therefor", Flame-Eye continued "you shouldn't kill the crow. A thief can become a benefactor and a supplicant an ally. Because the crow was badly treated he will help us all the more, and once we discover the weak points of our enemy, we will destroy him. Remember how, if there be discord in the enemy's ranks, life was granted by the thief and cows by the ghost." "How was that?" asked the Owl-King, and the counselor told this story.

The Brahmin, the Thief and the Demon Ghost

There was a very poor Brahmin who lived on alms that people gave him. It was a hard life. He looked terrible. He was disheveled and unhealthy for he had to live on the street year round in the heat, cold and rain. One day a rich farmer took pity on him and gave him two calves. The Brahmin managed, even though he begged others for his own food, to raise them well and they became quite plump. The two cows became his life-line.

One day, a thief saw the two cows and at once made plans to steal them from the Brahmin. So that night, the Thief got some thick rope and started walking in the direction where the Brahmin lived with the cows. On his way, he met a horrible looking creature with deformed body and fearsome eyes. He looked like he had escaped from purgatory. The Thief was scared and asked "Who are you?" and the other replied "I am a Demon Ghost and try to get at the truth. Now it is your turn to explain yourself." The Thief answered truthfully "I am a Thief and cruel. I am on my way to steal two cows from a poor Brahmin." The Demon Ghost laughed and said "I will join you. I eat every three days and it is eating-day today. I am hungry and will eat this Brahmin. Let us go." So together they walked to the Brahmin's shack and waited around until he was sound asleep.

Then the Demon Ghost made the first move towards the Brahmin but the Thief stopped him. "Hey! Wait a minute. This is not right. You cannot attack the Brahmin to begin eating him until I have removed the cows." But the Demon Ghost said "The noise you will make tying up the cows and getting them out will wake the Brahmin and he will escape." The Thief replied "If something happens when you try to eat the poor Brahmin, I will not be able to steal the cows." So the enemies of the Brahmin began to argue among themselves.

The Brahmin heard them and watched with half-closed eyes. Seeing the Demon Ghost, he first said a prayer for deliverance to his favorite God. And as the Demon Ghost began to disappear, the Brahmin picked up a cudgel and saved his two cows from the Thief.

*

"Besides" continued the counselor to the Owl-King, it is written in the scriptures that it is wrong to kill a supplicant. Do not kill the Crow." The Owl-King turned to yet another counselor "What do you say?" The counselor, named Wall-Eared, said "You should certainly not kill the Crow. If you spare his life, you may well grow to like him and become friends. But remember also that *it is better to keep secrets in the give and take of mutual defense* or perish like the snake in the belly and the snake in the ant-hill." "Please explain." said the Owl-King, and the counselor told this story.

The Snake in the Prince's Belly

In a city-state called Janga lived a King named Divine. He had a son who was wasting away because he had a parasite snake who lived in his belly. The Prince was very depressed because he could not live a normal life and that made his parents very sad. So he left the city and went to another city in another state and there he lived on alms and spent most of time in a big temple.

The King of that city, named Offering, had two daughters. One bowed daily to her father saying "Victory to you, O King" while the other greeted him with "Just Deserts, Dear King". The King was first irritated by the second daughter and eventually got very angry with her for persisting with her greeting. He ordered his ministers to give her to some foreigner so *she* would get her just deserts. And so they gave her to the Prince who was an outsider and lived simply in the temple.

The young bride was un-phased. She happily accepted the Prince as her husband and together they left to go to another place far away from her family. There they found a house by the edge of a pond. The Prince stayed in the yard while the Princess went grocery shopping with their one servant. When she came home she found the Prince asleep with his head resting on an ant-hill. From his mouth emerged the head of a hooded snake taking the air and looking directly at another snake which was emerging from the ant-hill. Both snakes were angry at each other. The ant-hill snake said "You villain! How can you torment this poor Prince by living in his belly?" And the other said "How come you hoard two pots of gold in your ant-hill?" They kept arguing for a while. The ant-hill snake said "If the Prince just drank black mustard oil, he could easily get rid of you!" and the belly-snake replied "Boiling water poured in the ant-hill would destroy you!"

As it happened, the Princess had overheard the snake arguments and since they had revealed each other's weak points, she was happy. She proceeded to use the methods the snakes had themselves mentioned to destroy them both. In so doing she made her husband well, acquired quite a large fortune in gold, and returned home to live happily ever after. She had her just deserts.

*

The Owl-King was finally convinced to spare the life of the Crow Live-Strong. But the counselor Red-Eye was displeased and said to the other counselors "Our master is ruined by your bad advice. It does not make sense to forgive a clear offence. Remember how the carpenter was duped by his faithless wife and her wicked lover?" "How was that?" asked the counselors, and Red-Eye told this story.

The Carpenter Duped By His Wicked Wife

There was a Carpenter married to an unfaithful wife. The whole village knew that she was a bad woman and rumors had reached the Carpenter. So one day, he started off to test her fidelity. He told her that he was going to a neighboring village on a two-day job and would she please pack him enough food to take with him which she did very willingly.

The minute the Carpenter left, his wife sent a message to her lover that she was free and asked him to come over that night. Meanwhile the Carpenter returned home and sneaked into the bedroom and hid under the bed.

That night the wife's lover went to bed first. So the Carpenter knew his wife was unfaithful. But still he waited and remained hidden to see what would happen. As the wife was about to get into bed, she accidentally kicked something under the bed. She immediately grasped the true situation. Her husband had set a trap and she had walked into it! But she was a clever harlot. So she stood by the bed and asked her lover to listen. "I am a good woman and love my husband. I asked you to come here because this morning the fortune-teller told me that my husband's life is in danger and that the only way to avert widowhood is for me to debase myself with another man. Please remember that is the only reason why I am ready to make love to you."

The lover understood what the wife was trying to hint and he played along and had fun making love. The stupid, gullible, good Carpenter swallowed the deception hook, line and sinker, and ran all over the village singing their praises. Everyone, of course, laughed behind his back.

*

"That is why I say" continued Red-Eye "shrewd men try to unmask a foe who seems a friend." But the other counselors disregarded his wisdom and picked up Live-Strong to take him to the Owl-King's fortress.

Live-Strong then asked the Owl-King "Why are you so kind to me O King? I have done nothing yet to deserve it. Please place me in your debt forever by sitting me near a fire." Red-Eye suspected something was up and asked "Why do you wish to be close to a fire?" Live-Strong replied "I was beaten nearly to death for your sake. Now all I want is to cleanse myself in the fire and be reborn as an owl to take revenge on the crows." Red-Eye, a master of diplomacy, countered with "Even if born as an owl, you would find the crows sympathetic and a kindred kind, for no-one forgets one's origins. Remember the mouse-maid? Even though the mouse-turned- girl had suitors like the sun, cloud, wind and mountain, she chose a mouse and reverted to her own natural species." "Please explain" said Live-Strong, and Red-Eye told this story.

Once a Mouse, Always a Mouse

There was once a holy man who lived by the shores of a mighty river that cascaded down high mountains. The Holy Man had magical powers but he lived simply with his wife within a community of like-minded pious people. The Wife had no children which made her sad. One day, as the Holy Man was bathing in the river a tiny but beautiful baby mouse fell from the claws of a hawk flying overhead right into his hands. He looked at the baby mouse, wondered what he should do, thought about his Wife, and decided to change the baby mouse into a little baby girl and took her home. His Wife was delighted and raised her as her own daughter until she became of marriageable age.

When the time came, the Wife said to her husband "It is time for our daughter to marry. Please find a suitable husband for her." The Holy Man thought it is important to give her in marriage to someone of her own station. Where wealth is comparable and the family status the same, marriages work out well, but it never works between rich and poor. Seven things are needed for a successful marriage: money, good looks, learning, good family, youth, position and virtue. So, if she agrees, I will give her to the Sun who lights up the whole world. "No Father," said the Girl. "He is too burning hot. Please find another."

So the Holy Man asked the Sun "Is there anyone superior to you?" "Yes", said the Sun, "the Cloud. When he gets in front of me, I disappear." "No Father," said the Girl "The Cloud is too dark and frigid. Please find another." So the Holy Man asked the Cloud "Is there anyone superior to you?" "Yes," said the Cloud "The Wind. He can blow me away." "No Father," said the Girl "The Wind is too restless and flighty. Please find another." So the Holy Man asked the Wind "Is there anyone superior to you?" "Yes," said the Wind "the Mountain. No one can move him." "No Father," said the Girl "the Mountain is stiff and rough all over. Please find another." So the Holy Man asked the Mountain "Is there anyone superior to you?" "Yes," said the Mountain "the Mouse. He can make holes in my entire body." "Yes, please" said the Girl. I would be happy to wed a mouse." So the Holy Man turned her back into a mouse and she lived happily married to a mouse husband.

*

But no one listened to Red-Eye's story or paid attention to the point of it. The owls took the Crow to their fortress and on the flight Live-Strong had a good laugh. He thought 'they could have and should have killed me without having to pay any price.'

When they reached the fortress the Owl-King said to his servants "Give the Crow the room he prefers. He is a well-wisher of ours." Quickly, Live-Strong figured out that in order to destroy the fortress he would need to stay near the entrance. So he said to the Owl-King "O King, I am a well-wisher but I also know my place. I must not presume to stay in the heart of the fortress. I will stay near the entrance and pay homage daily from here." The Owl-King agreed and let Live-Strong live near the entrance gate of the owl fortress where the servants took good care of the Crow.

But Red-Eye, seeing how Live-Strong was being pampered, was disturbed and said to the Owl-King and his counselors "You are all being taken in. Remember the song "I played the fool first, followed by he who tethered me, then king and counselor. We were all fools together." "How so?" asked a counselor, and Red-Eye told this story.

The Bird with Gold Droppings

There was a very big tree on the side of a very high mountain in which lived a bird with gold droppings.

One day a hunter who was also an accomplished fowler was passing by when directly in front of him the bird dropping fell to the ground. It had turned golden the moment it came out of the Bird. The Hunter was amazed. He had never seen such a phenomenon in his entire life! So he set a snare and the foolish Bird got caught immediately. Then the Hunter took the Bird out of the snare, put him in a cage, and took him home.

But the Hunter was very worried because it seemed to him the Bird could be an ill omen. If other people saw the Bird's peculiar dropping of gold, they would be sure to report him to the King and his very life could be forfeit. So he decided to take the Bird to the King himself.

When the King saw the Bird and heard the Hunter's story, he was pleased. He told his attendants to care for the Bird, give him plenty to eat and drink. "Why do you keep the Bird, O King?" asked a counselor. "He was hatched from an ordinary egg. You have only the Hunter's word of this Bird's gold droppings. You have no other proof. Have you ever known gold in a bird dropping? Set the Bird free." The King was gullible and took his counselor's advice and set the Bird free.

At which point the Bird flew up to a high parapet in the palace, alighted, made a dropping of gold and flew away singing "First me, then Hunter, then King, then Counselor. All fools together."

But no one paid any attention to the point of Red-Eye's story and advice. They continued to pamper Live-Strong who was now completely recovered from his beating by the Crow King Spirit. Finally, Red-Eye gathered his personal staff and said to them in private "The end is at hand. The King and fortress will soon be in ruins. I have given my best advice but the Owl-King will not listen. So it is now time for us to seek another fortress. Planning ahead is so much better than getting caught unawares. Remember the cave that talked?" "How was that?" asked his staff, and Red-Eye told this story.

The Talking Cave

There was a deep cave in a mountain side where a jackal named Planner lived. He was a very careful jackal and always checked to see whether the cave was safe to enter. One day, as the sun was about to set, a Lion named Crusher, was passing by the same cave. He thought to himself some animal is bound to come into the cave for shelter at night, so I will hide just inside and wait. When the Jackal returned he called out "O Cave, O Cave, How goes it?" He waited a while and then called out again "O Cave, why won't you speak to me? We had a deal that when I come to you and called out, you would answer me promptly." Again he waited for a while and said "OK, I will go to the other Cave who will probably be more polite than you." Upon hearing the Jackal, the Lion thought to himself the Cave is not answering because he senses I am here and is afraid to do so. I will answer the Jackal's greeting myself and when he enters make a meal of him. So the Lion roared a greeting which echoed greatly in the cave and terrified all creatures who heard it. The Jackal, of course, fled, thinking it is always wise to know what to fear and plan ahead.

"So" said Red-Eye to his staff "Come with me" and they all left in search of a safe home. Live-Strong was delighted to see them go. He knew Red-Eye was learned and far-sighted and could have been a problem because the shrewd counselor can discover enemies disguised as friends. Meanwhile, as each day passed, Live-Strong collected an ember from the forest fires and hid it in his own nest. The Owls had no idea about what he was up to. He just seemed to be building a nest but Live-Strong had collected quite a woodpile at the fortress gate. Every morning, when the owls turned blind, he went out and made a report to his own King Spirit to fill him in on what he was doing. One day, he was ready and said to King Spirit "I have made the enemy's cave ready for burning. Please come quickly with all your retinue with each crow bringing a lighted stick to throw on my nest at the entrance to the owl fortress. Then all your enemies will burn to death. Please be quick, there is no time to lose." King Spirit followed Live-Strong's advice to the letter and the crows exterminated the owls and returned safely to their home in the banyan tree.

Once enthroned comfortably, King Spirit asked Live-Strong to recount his time in the enemy camp. "Most of the owls were a pack of fools" replied Live-Strong, but one, Red-Eye, had great intelligence, learning and insight, and correctly gauged my purpose and strategy. But the other counselors were dimwits even as they pretended to give sage advice to the Owl-King. And the Owl-King was not at all aware that *a prudent ruler guards himself by being well-advised. The steady forfeit glory, the restless forfeit friends, the bankrupt forfeit family, the bankers forfeit wealth, the passionate forfeit learning, the careless forfeit followers, and the kings forfeit kingly power - all because of taking bad advice.* My time in the enemy camp was a test of endurance but in the end it paid off. Remember the great black snake killed all the frogs." "How was that?" asked King Spirit, and Live-Strong told this story.

Frogs That Rode On The Back of Snake

Once, an old black snake called Fang was sun-bathing on a rock and taking stock of his life. He was now pretty old and was having trouble catching prey comfortably. So he decided on a plan and went to a nearby pond where there were many frogs. He lay about on the edge of the water looking obviously very depressed. Seeing him do nothing a curious frog approached near and asked him "How come you are not hunting for food?" "I am in real trouble" replied Fang. "Earlier this evening, I was going to creep up on a frog but he saw me in time and hopped into the middle of a group of holy men and their families. I tried to follow the frog but mistakenly bit a Brahmin boy's toe which looked like a frog. The boy died. The father Brahmin was so angry that he put a curse on me. "You killed an innocent boy who did you no harm" he cried. "You will be damned from now on and will be completely dependent on the frogs. You will be a vehicle for the frogs and they will ride your back. And you will live only on whatever the frogs allow you to eat." "So you see" said Fang "I am undone."

The curious frog, satisfied that he had heard the truth, repeated the amazing story to all other frogs in the pond. They were delighted to hear that the black snake they dreaded would now be their vehicle. So they all rode the snake that day. The next day Fang seemed very slow moving. So much so that the frog-King asked the Snake "Why are you not carrying me as well as you did yesterday? To which Fang replied "Because I am starving. You have not fed me anything at all." So the Frog-King allowed Fang to eat some small low-born frogs. But Fang did not stop there. He kept eating frogs until he grew really strong. He was very pleased with his trickery and wondered how long the frogs would last.

The very next day another black snake came by and saw Fang giving rides to frogs. Irritated, he asked Fang "Why are you carrying our natural food on your back?" Fang answered "I am simply marking time like the butter-blind Brahmin!" "How so?" asked the Snake, and Fang told this story.

The Revenge of the Brahmin

There was a Brahmin, named Believer, whose wife was unfaithful. She was always running after other men and often baked them cakes with lots of sugar and butter thereby short-changing her husband. One day, Believer saw her and asked "What are you making? And where do you take all the cakes you bake? Tell me the truth." The quick, clever, harlot had a ready lie: "There is a shrine of the blessed goddess nearby where I participate in a fasting ceremony and take delicious cakes as an offering." Then she left for the shrine but went first to the river for a cleansing bath.

The Brahmin, who had deliberately taken a different road , arrived at the shrine before his wife and proceeded to hide behind the Goddess statue. The wife appeared shortly thereafter having completed her obligatory rituals. She bowed to the Goddess and prayed "Please help me. How may I make my husband blind?" The Brahmin was stunned to hear his wife's prayer but with great presence of mind answered in a disguised voice "Feed him mostly butter and butter-cakes and he will eventually go blind." Sure enough the Wife began feeding her husband butter and butter-cakes and after a few days Believer said to his Wife "I don't see too well. I may be going blind" hearing which the Wife thanked the Goddess in her heart.

Meanwhile, the Wife's lover began visiting her at her home daily because he too thought the husband had gone blind and so he had nothing to fear. However, after a fortnight or so, the Brahmin was ready for his revenge. When the Lover came, he picked up a cudgel and clubbed him to death. Then he cut of his Wife's nose so the whole village would know her infidelity.

*

When Fang finished telling the story, the other snake took off. Needless to say, when Fang had bided his time sufficiently, he ate up all the frogs in the pond.

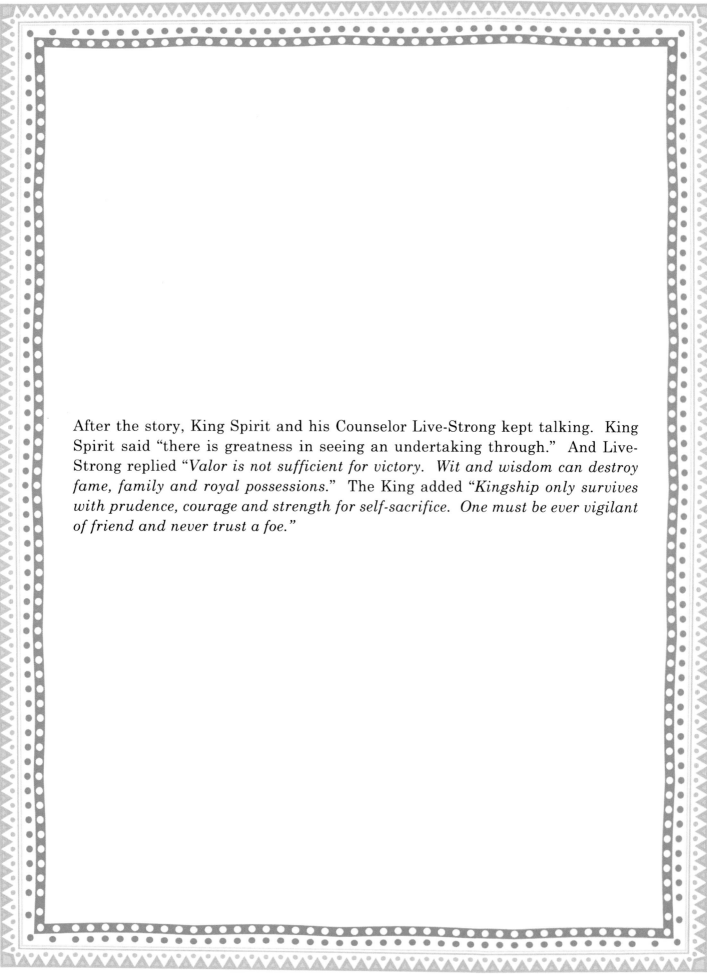

After the story, King Spirit and his Counselor Live-Strong kept talking. King Spirit said "there is greatness in seeing an undertaking through." And Live-Strong replied *"Valor is not sufficient for victory. Wit and wisdom can destroy fame, family and royal possessions."* The King added *"Kingship only survives with prudence, courage and strength for self-sacrifice. One must be ever vigilant of friend and never trust a foe."*

ACKNOWLEDGEMENTS

As I have noted elsewhere, the *Panchatantra* stories (literally Five Books) have been part of India's oral and scholarly tradition for at least two thousand years or more. They have been told and retold all over the world and have influenced many literary genres, particularly those containing animal characters and 'nesting stories' i.e. one story in another story in another story. Sometime towards the end of the twelfth century, the seminal version of the *Panchatantra* was written by Vishnusharma in Sanskrit and has formed the best known rendition ever since. It is comprised of a vast array of folk wisdom interspersed with eighty-five stories which collectively serve as a guide book of sorts on how to live a wise and good life. Many translations of the text are available in English and some selected stories have been published for young children. However, the entire collection has never been adapted for casual readers, whether teenagers or adults.

My goal is to make the core of the *Panchatantra* easily accessible to the English speaking world. I have delved deeply into three authoritative, literal, translations of the complete text of the *Panchatantra* from the original Sanskrit by three eminent scholars: Arthur W. Rider (1925), Chandra Rajan (1993) and Patrick Olivelle (1997). Their work represents the best of what serious academics have to offer. I am clearly indebted to them. Nevertheless, the original in its entirety remains rather difficult to register and enjoy for non-academics. I have used their translations to understand and stay as close to the original of the *Panchatantra* as possible. Beyond that, the way I have organized the five books for a lay audience, the telling of the stories, the language used, and the summary of the wisdom highlighted by the stories, are entirely mine.

I have read and re-read the stories in various forms over the last fifty years. I wish I had a way of publicly thanking all the authors I have read on the subject of the Panchatantra. Suffice it to say, their work taught me that these ancient stories are the essence of Indian wisdom and values that deserve a wide international audience.

Throughout this venture, my husband Michael has been my strongest backer, my sharpest critic, my meticulous editor, and my most longsuffering love. I cannot thank him enough. I also owe thanks to my children, Kieran and Sean, who never failed to point out that my stories were not PC enough for children, and to my friends, Roland, Judy and Jon, who did not hesitate to point out that my story-telling was too confusing even for adults. I hope they will see that I took their judgments seriously.

I hope that my enthusiasm for these stories is catching. Cheers.

Narindar Uberoi Kelly, June 2014

MORE TALL TALES OF OLD INDIA

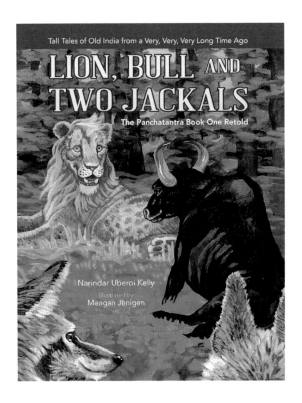

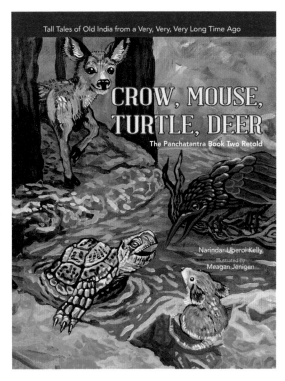

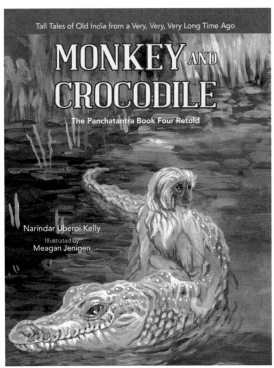

The Panchatantra Retold
Narindar Uberoi Kelly
Illustrated by Meagan Jenigen

CPSIA information can be obtained
at www.ICGtesting.com
Printed in the USA
BVXC01n1632210714
359734BV00001B/2

9 781490 740409